Copyright © 2009 by Jim LaMarche.
All rights reserved. No part of this book may be reproduced in any
form without written permission from the publisher.

Book design by Jim LaMarche and Amelia May Anderson.
Handlettering by Carl Rohrs.
The illustrations in this book were rendered in acrylic washes and
colored pencil on Arches watercolor paper.
Manufactured in China.

Library of Congress Cataloging-in-Publication Data
LaMarche, Jim.
Lost and found / Jim LaMarche.
p. cm.
Summary: Three stories about being lost, being found, finding home,
and, most importantly, about the dogs that help us find the way.
ISBN 978-0-8118-6401-5
1. Children's stories, American. 2. Dogs—Juvenile fiction. [1. Dogs—
Fiction. 2. Lost children—Fiction. 3. Lost and found possessions—
Fiction. 4. Short stories.] I. Title.
PZ7.L15957Lo 2009
[E]—dc22
2008023009

10 9 8 7 6 5 4 3 2

Chronicle Books LLC
680 Second Street, San Francisco, California 94107

www.chroniclekids.com

# LOST and FOUND

## THREE DOG STORIES
*by* Jim LaMarche

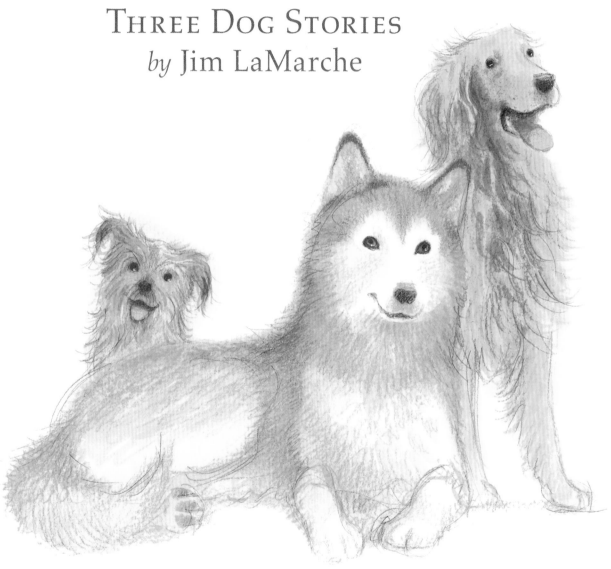

chronicle books · san francisco

For my father, who inspired the
Ginger story. And for my mother,
who inspires us all.

Molly

"That's enough sass!" said Anna's mother.
"You need a Time Out."

Anna slammed her door and flopped down
on her bed. "You're the only one who loves me,
Molly," she said. Then she had an idea.

"Sssshhh . . ."

"Come on, Molly."

Anna and Molly marched through the tall grass,
up a rocky hill, then into the woods.

They crossed a creek, climbed over boulders,

"We'll build our own house right here, Molly."

and hiked into the aspen grove.

Anna dragged big stones to make some walls.
She spread out aspen leaves to make a bed.

While Anna napped, Molly watched.

Molly's bark woke Anna up.

"What are you barking at, Molly? There's nothing out there."
Anna looked all around her. The sky was getting dark.

"I think we should go home now, Molly."

But which way was home?

Then Anna had an idea. "Home, Molly," she said. "Please, go home." Molly sniffed the ground.

Anna followed Molly through the aspens, back over the boulders,

She sniffed the air. Then she looked back at Anna and wagged her tail.

across the creek, and out of the woods,

until, at last,

they were home!

Ginger

"Wake up, Ginger." Jules scratched Ginger behind her ear. She loved that.

"Oh, Jules," said Mom. "Why do you let Ginger sleep on your jacket? You're going to smell like a dog."

"Good," said Jules. "I want to smell like Ginger."

"Rise and shine," Dad called. "The pancakes are almost ready. And we have a perfect day for our hike."

Jules got dressed while
Dad packed their lunch.

"Jump, Ginger!"

"You two dogs are going to
get bugs in your teeth."

Jules and Ginger leaped
out of the truck running.

It was a perfect day.

They hiked all morning on their favorite trail. At the
creek, they ate tuna sandwiches and drank cold lemonade.
Then they looked for the smoothest stones.

Suddenly something
caught Ginger's eye.

"Ginger, STOP!" cried Jules. But Ginger didn't stop.

"Ginger, STAY!" yelled Dad. But Ginger was off.

Jules and his dad quickly put on their socks and shoes and scrambled up the bank, but Ginger was gone.

Together they called, "One, two, three, GINGER!" They listened. Nothing.

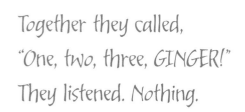

They searched deep into the woods. But there was no sign of Ginger.

After hours of looking, Dad stopped and knelt down.
"Jules, we have to start back," he said.

"But Dad, we can't leave Ginger here!" cried Jules.

"We'll start looking again at dawn," said Dad.
"We'll find Ginger. I promise."

By the time they got back to the truck, the sun
had set. Without a word they climbed in and
started down the road.

"Dad! Stop! Stop!" Jules jumped
out of the truck and ran back
to the edge of the woods.

He spread out his jacket in the grass.

Jules worried all through the night. Was Ginger frightened?
Was she safe? Would she find his jacket?

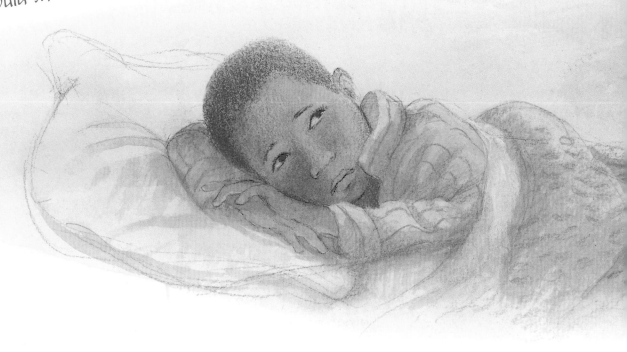

Jules and his dad drove back to the woods at dawn.

Jules ran through the high grass.

"GINGER! GINGER?" he yelled.

At the sound of his voice, Ginger popped her head up from her warm bed.

Ginger was found.

Yuki

"Hey, don't eat that!" said Jack. He searched around in his backpack until he found half a bologna sandwich. He held it out to the dog. "Here," he said. "Try this."

The dog scarfed down the sandwich in one bite.

"You must be starving," said Jack. "What's your name, boy?" He checked the dog's collar. "Yuki. Well, come on, Yuki. You can come home with me."

"Mom! Look what I found!" Jack shouted.

"Oh, my," said Mom.

"Can we keep him? I'll feed him and walk him. He won't be any trouble."

"He can't stay here, Jack," said Mom. "There's no room in the trailer, and we can't afford to feed him. Besides, this dog belongs to someone. He's a purebred."

"Pleeease, Mom," said Jack.

"I'm sorry, Jack," said Mom. "Someday, when I find a job and we get a nice place, I promise you we'll get a dog."

That evening, Jack made a FOUND poster.

In the morning, they made copies
of it at the library.

Then they posted the signs around
the neighborhood.

Nobody came to claim Yuki on the first day . . .

. . . or the second . . .

. . . or the third.

By the end of the week, it looked like no one would claim Yuki.

"You're gonna be mine, boy," Jack whispered.

And then, one morning, an old woman came to the door.

"Yuki?"

"Yuki!"

"This is Mrs. Merino," said Mom.

"Thank you so much for taking care of Yuki, Jack," said Mrs. Merino. "I was so worried about him. He was really my husband's dog, you see. The two of them spent every day together in Joe's studio—until Joe died. I think Yuki runs off looking for his old friend."

"He's a great dog," said Jack.

"It looks like he feels the same about you," said Mrs. Merino.

Mrs. Merino looked at Jack and Yuki, then at the little trailer. "Would you be interested in a job?" she asked Mom.

So Jack and Mom moved into Mr. Merino's studio. Mom went to work cooking and cleaning for Mrs. Merino.

And Jack and Yuki?

Well, Yuki never ran away again.